# FRED FLINTSTONE:
# THE FIX-IT

Story by

Distributed by
**WONDER BOOKS • NEW YORK**
**A Division of GROSSET & DUNLAP, Inc.**
Published by Ottenheimer Publishers, Inc.

One Sunday morning Fred and Wilma Flintstone were having breakfast when the toaster stopped working. Wilma said she would

take it to a shop that did repairs, but Fred said,
"NOT on your life! I know exactly what'll happen!
They'll charge us a fortune to fix it, and when we
get it back, it'll be no better than it is right now!
I'll fix it myself! Easy as pie!"

Fred took the toaster and went down to the cellar, where he kept a few tools. He was down there for a couple of hours, humming and singing while he worked. Finally, he came upstairs, carrying the toaster.

"All fixed, dear?" asked Wilma.

"Not quite," answered Fred. "I'm not sure it's the toaster. It may be some trouble with the house wiring. I'll get Barney over here to help. We may have to change things around a little!"

Not long afterward, Barney arrived, said, "Hi, Wilma! Where's the genius? In the cellar?" Wilma said, "That's where he is, Barney." Barney

gave Pebbles a pat on the head and trotted downstairs.

Wilma picked up her sewing basket and sat

down in the living room to catch up on her mending. A few minutes later she heard lots of arguing going on. Then Barney came up the steps and went into the attic. At the same time, Fred appeared and went out the front door. Wilma could

hear them yelling back and forth at each other — things like, "No, not THAT one — THIS one!" And, "Disconnect that blue wire and connect the yellow one, but be careful it doesn't touch the red!" Then there was a yell and a thump, and Fred fell off the roof. He bounced right up again, ran into the attic, and then there were more sounds and yelling back and forth.

After another half hour, Fred and Barney went

down to the cellar again. In another fifteen minutes, they both came back up. Fred handed the
toaster to Wilma.

"All fixed," he said. "Good as new!"

"Does it work?" asked Wilma.

"Plug it in," said Barney, with a satisfied grin.

Wilma plugged in the toaster and turned it on. Immediately, it began a strange humming sound, and a white foam oozed out of the slots where toast was supposed to pop up.

"What the—" cried Fred. Barney looked closely at the toaster and the white foamy stuff, stuck his finger in it, and tasted it. His face took on a strange look.

"Well? What IS that stuff?" asked Fred.

"Hot lather! Freddie, you've got a great invention here! This is the only toaster in the world you can shave with!" Barney began to laugh so hard, he had to hold his sides.

"Just be quiet!" yelled Fred. "I'll take it to be fixed tomorrow! Wilma, turn on the rockavision. There's a good Western on that I want to see!"

Wilma turned on the rockavision set, but nothing happened.

"Hey, Fred!" cried Barney. "Doesn't it feel cold in here?"

"What's the matter with the set?" growled
Fred. He walked around to the back and let out a
yell. "Hey! No wonder it's cold in here! Look!"

Barney and Wilma looked. The inside of the
rockavision set was one solid pile of ice cubes!

Just at that moment, Pebbles was playing with
Wilma's vacuum cleaner, where Wilma had left it
after cleaning up some crumbs from dinner the

night before. With no warning at all, slices of
toast came popping out of the vacuum cleaner!

"Hey, folks!" cried Barney. "This is some house!
The toaster makes hot lather, the rockavision set
is full of ice cubes, and the vacuum cleaner is
turning out toast! What next?"

"Never mind!" grunted Fred. "I'm gonna get a cold drink from the refrigerator!"

"Bring me one!" called Barney, as Fred went
into the kitchen.

Ten seconds later, Wilma and Barney heard a blast of music coming from the kitchen. They ran out there, and saw Fred sitting on the floor, staring at the open refrigerator. That's where the loud music was coming from!

Barney disconnected the refrigerator and the

music stopped. "Freddie," he said, "you can do one of two things. Keep on the way you're going, if you can remember which gadget does what. Or you can call in an electrician and get things back to normal. I'm going back home. See you at the rock mine in the morning!"

At the door, Barney turned and said, "Oh, by the way, I wouldn't use your electric razor in the morning, if I were you. The way things are around here, it would have to be the sewing machine that will give you a nice close shave!"